HAUNTED SECRETS
TALES OF
ELOISE
VOLUME 1

SCARE STREET

ISBN: 979-8-89476-067-4
Copyright © 2024 by ScareStreet.com

ENTER THE REALM OF TERROR...

We'd like to take a moment to thank you for your support and invite you to join our VIP newsletter.

Dive deeper into the darkness with exclusive offers, early access to new releases, and bone-chilling deals when you sign up at www.ScareStreet.com.

Let the nightmares begin…

See you in the shadows,
Scare Street

Table of Contents

FRENEMIES

Eloise was not supposed to be in the cellar; Shane Ryan had made that very clear many times now. However, he was not always home, and he had no idea what it was like in the house when he was not home. It was not very easy to find something to do.

Something about the dark ones in the cellar drew her any time Shane was gone for more than a few days. They whispered down there, and she could hear them in the walls when she was very still and alone.

She had to get away from Thaddeus and the others to hear them, especially the Davis sisters with whom she very much enjoyed playing most of but not all the time. They were good at games sometimes, but not always. They didn't always let Eloise win either, and that upset her. She liked to win. They could also get too loud and too close, and she needed to be alone in the dark and quiet sometimes, too.

The dark ones were so much different from the ones who lived in the rest of the house. and maybe that was why she found them so exciting. Even the name "dark ones" was enticing. It was meant to make her curious, she was certain.

Carl said they were not to be spoken to because they had nothing good to say. They drifted in shadows from here to there and were obsessed with dark deeds and dark thoughts and other very dramatic things. Carl was very serious and very boring.

Thaddeus did not like to play with the dark ones at all, and he was also very boring sometimes. Eloise knew she would not be friends with Thaddeus if she didn't have to be, and even then, it was very trying sometimes. She liked to play games with him that she knew she would win, but he grew tired of them and gave up too easily. Her favorite was hide and seek because she liked catching him when he was so sure he was safe and hidden. She always knew his secrets. Eloise liked knowing secrets.

Everyone wanted to treat Eloise like a child, but she was old. She was very old now, and everyone forgot that because she couldn't grow. She was dead. And being dead also meant many things were far less dangerous than everyone, including Shane Ryan, seemed to think.

Eloise was not naïve. She understood what danger was. Everyone else just didn't understand her.

She could do whatever she wanted. She wouldn't say that out loud, of course. But she thought it. Why shouldn't she do what she wanted when she wanted? Who would get hurt?

These were the words she told herself as she ventured down through shadows and corners and quiet places in the house.

She had found a spot in the cellar that was right below the back part of the house. Inches of wood separated it from the outside and the sun. The house could change sometimes. It would hide rooms, or move them here and there, but not this place. This place was always the same, and it allowed her to go from the sunlight to the darkness in the blink of an eye. And that was where she met Gerald.

At first, she would just drop into her spot, her little shielded cubby, and watch the dark ones. It was like a zoo, she thought. They crept and slithered and darted about and paid her little mind. Day by day, however, it became clear that they saw her there. They knew.

She would only catch a glance in the beginning. One would watch her, dead eyes transfixed, and when she saw it, it would vanish. She was not interesting to them, for she was as dead as they were and could offer very little. They wanted to play with Shane Ryan, or sometimes his friends that came to the house to see him.

Then, things changed slowly. One would linger when the others darted away. He held eye contact for just a heartbeat at first, until one day, longer. They stared at one another in the dark, and the others receded until it was only him and Eloise.

"Hello. My name is Eloise, what's yours?"

He did not reply. He vanished, darkness into darkness, so she left to play with the sisters.

The next time she returned, their staring match resumed.

"I will call you Gerald," she told him, and this time, he did not flee. She took that to mean she had guessed his name correctly. "What do you do down here, Gerald?"

He didn't answer, he just stared. Unlike the sisters and Carl and Thaddeus, Gerald didn't have a real shape. He was not a man or a boy or anything; he was just a shadow with a face. It was sort of a man's face, she thought. It moved sometimes, the way shadows did, and was hard to describe. His eyes were black in black, but they glowed, too. Like a cat, she thought, and that made her smile.

"You will never believe what Shane Ryan has done," she announced to Gerald one day after Shane had come home from some adventure to a faraway place. She heard him telling Carl what had transpired, and now she told Gerald because it was very exciting and full of danger. Shane Ryan had so much freedom, and she envied him that.

Gerald listened and did not interrupt because he was a good listener. Thaddeus interrupted stories when Eloise told them, and sometimes, the sisters just spoke over her. Carl knew all the stories already and didn't care to listen at all.

She would go down to her dark corner now and then when she got bored or lonely and would talk to Gerald because he was always there and always waiting. When she asked him questions, he would not speak, so she eventually gave up asking and only spoke to him. The others would silence their whispers, and Eloise would talk and talk for as long as she dared.

Only so much time could be spared with the dark ones, for inevitably, someone would come looking for her. Carl or the sisters or even Shane

Ryan, though this was very rare. She would slip away and be happy knowing Gerald would always keep her secret because he never spoke.

Until he did.

"Stay."

He said it when she finished a story about something that had come in the mail for Shane that had a ghost pirate hidden inside. It was very exciting for about ten minutes. She was ready to leave again when Gerald had made his request.

His voice was softer than she expected. It was like a sigh. Like words people speak when they are not fully awake. His glowing eyes were fixed and unblinking and stared into her own. He was closer now than he had been before. Not close enough to touch, but close.

"What for?" she asked.

Her story was done, so staying didn't make much sense. She had nothing else to say, and Gerald would only stare in silence otherwise, and that was very boring, even if he didn't realize it.

He didn't answer, so she left. Gerald was a good listener, but he needed to learn how to say what he wanted to say if he wanted to be a better friend.

Some days, Eloise would not visit Gerald. Sometimes, she just had nothing to say. Once, she forgot to visit for a whole year. But whenever she returned with new stories, he was in almost the same place. Almost. He was getting closer.

"Where do you go when you leave?" he asked her one time. The question caught her off-guard because it was an entire question, and it was his first ever.

"Home. Into the house," she replied.

"Home?"

"Home. I live upstairs with Shane Ryan and Carl and the others. You live down here with your friends."

"Friends…" Gerald whispered. It did not sound like a question, but she began to wonder if it was.

"I don't go upstairs," Gerald replied.

"Why not? What's stopping you?" Eloise said.

That the dark ones were dangerous and kept in the cellar did not explain why they stayed in the cellar. She was not sure what kept them down there.

One of Eloise's greatest disappointments was that she could not go everywhere she wanted to. She was jealous of the people who got to go out into the world with Shane Ryan on his adventures. They could go anywhere in the whole wide world, and that was something she longed for very much. She could go some places, even out of the house. But not everywhere.

The people who came to the house did not appreciate their freedom, she thought. They seemed to squander it very often. It made her want to scream at them.

"Why are you in this house?" she wanted to yell. "Go to all the other houses!"

She would go to every house if she could. Every house in every country all over the world. But she lost that ability a long time ago, and now it was only a silly dream that could never be real. Sometimes, that made her angry.

"I want to come with you," Gerald suggested.

"What do you mean?"

"Let me... live in the house. Like you."

"Oh," Eloise said. Surely Gerald could have left on his own any time if he'd wanted to. He didn't need her to help him with that.

She left the cellar because Gerald was being silly, and she didn't enjoy it. She liked it better when all he did was listen.

She waited many days before she returned to the cellar because she needed Gerald to think about what he'd done, even if she'd never explicitly told him to.

When she returned, he was not there.

She sat in her corner, the place where she felt safe, and watched the dark ones moving from shadow to shadow. But none of them stayed and looked at her with more than a fleeting glance, so she left without a word.

Shane Ryan came home from somewhere, and she listened intently while he explained what was happening in his life to Carl. Someone had hurt him badly, but he was better now, at least a little bit. But he had to go again, and Eloise was certain he was leaving to kill the people who had wronged him. That was the right thing to do, she thought. Bad people could not just be left to run loose.

While she listened from the hallway near the kitchen, something caught her eye. A shadow, outside of the kitchen, beyond where Carl and Shane Ryan could see. Maybe they wouldn't have even seen it if they looked right at it, but Eloise saw it because she knew what to look for.

Gerald had left the cellar. He was in the house where he said he never went. In the dark, she saw his glowing eyes look into her. There was nothing else to see, but she knew he was smiling, and it made her angry. He told her he never went upstairs, and now here he was. He had lied to her, and that wasn't nice.

"You said you didn't come upstairs," she said in a very quiet whisper.

"I came here for you," Gerald replied, his sigh of a voice barely reaching her ears.

"I went looking for you to talk, and you weren't there."

"Because I'm here," he said.

She turned her back on him and ignored what Shane Ryan and Carl were saying. She liked that Gerald stayed put in the cellar. She liked that he listened to her, and secretly, she liked that he didn't talk back or go away or ignore her. At least, that was what he used to do.

When she looked back, he was gone. She did not think he had returned to the cellar, though. Why did he have to ruin things by coming upstairs? She wondered if it was her fault. She had asked what was stopping

6

him from coming up. Was that all it was? He just needed someone to ask? Shane Ryan would be very mad at her if he found out she'd invited Gerald upstairs.

She moved through the walls, through empty rooms no one had visited in many years, through cobwebs and corners and dusty, old spaces. She found him on the third floor, alone in a bedroom, creeping under a bed.

"What are you doing?" she asked.

"Don't you like it?" he said, his voice soft.

"Like what?"

"Being free," he replied. "Doing whatever you wish."

She was still cross with him for not listening, but his question made her think of what it must be like for Gerald and the others in the cellar. They were even less free than she was, and that had to be very boring sometimes.

"I'm not completely free," she said. "There are still rules."

"Don't go into the cellar," Gerald teased. He was just a shadow under the bed, a faint silhouette to be overlooked from the corner of your eyes.

"And other rules," she pointed out.

Eloise liked rules that could be broken sometimes. Those ones made games more fun and unpredictable. What good was a game if everyone could predict the ending? That was a waste of time.

"Shouldn't break the rules," Gerald whispered, as though reading her mind.

A faint breeze stirred in the room where none should have existed. The door creaked shut behind her.

"Sometimes, rules are silly," Eloise countered.

The room got darker than it had been only a moment before. The window had become hazy, as though there was a fog behind it, and the light of day was having trouble piercing the barrier.

Gerald's shiny eyes slithered closer across the floor, reaching the edge

7

of the bed. They never blinked, not even once. The room grew darker still, and the window became as black as night.

"What are you doing?" Eloise asked.

"Playing a game," the other ghost replied. So soft. So gentle.

"What are the rules of your game?" she wanted to know.

The shadows crept in around her. The glowing eyes drifted closer.

"The only rule is I win," Gerald said, his whisper right in her ear.

Eloise smiled and let herself go. She had been in the house a very long time. She knew every room, and every room knew her. She was as much a part of the house as the wood of the floor on which she crouched.

It took no effort to be in the wood. To be through the wood. To pass from the bedroom to the hallway below. One moment she was with Gerald, the next she was not. Because Shane Ryan's house was her house, too.

Gerald appeared, a glimmer in the shadow in the corner of the hall.

"Tricky girl," he said.

She grinned and shrugged.

"You can't win a game that easily, Gerald," she told the other ghost. "You can't just say you win and then win. That's not how it works."

"I win," he repeated.

The shadows flowed from the corner like water, covering the hallway from floor to ceiling. When they reached where Eloise had been standing, she was already gone again.

Gerald caught up with her in another bedroom. She sat on the bed, her feet dangling over the edge.

"You're very slow, Gerald," she teased.

Eloise could play hide and seek like no one else. She always won. Even against the sisters, she always won that game. No one could hide from her. No one could find her if she didn't want them to. But Gerald didn't know that.

The darkness bubbled up around the bed like water rising in a bathtub.

8

It touched Eloise's legs and tried to grab hold. The shiny, dark eyes shifted, and the girl was gone again.

The soft voice hissed, barely a sound at all.

***

Gerald roamed from room to room. He avoided the other ghosts. He stayed secret and hidden. He moved in the walls and the floorboards. He crept without a sound. High and low he went, but he could not find the girl anywhere, even as the house moved and shifted around him, revealing new rooms and new spaces.

In time, he retreated and went deeper into the house. The girl would come to him again, he thought. Her childish curiosity would drive her to him again. To them, down in the dark. And when no one else in the house knew, when no one else could hear, he would draw her into the darkness forever. He could consume her. He would make her his own. Forever. It would last forever.

Down he crept to the cellar once more, to the place that was his true home. Down in the shadows and the cold where he waited. He drifted in and out of the darkness, seeing nothing and everything in the empty space where the others did the same, always not quite there, not quite part of the space in which they were held.

The little girl never stayed away for too long. He knew her enough now. Knew her mind, knew her patterns. She would not elude him the next time. He would show her a proper game. He would show her why breaking the rules was a bad idea.

"Gerald."

It was her voice, but very quiet. The softest whisper. He searched the darkness and could not find her. Bodiless, he drifted like a shark in the depths, searching for her.

He went to her corner, the place where she always appeared. The place she foolishly felt safe in. She was not there.

His eyes scanned around but there were only the others like him, hiding far away, watching and waiting as he so often had done before.

Hands pulled at him, small and insistent. They drew him up into the light of day, into the outside world under the light of the sun.

He writhed and twisted to escape, but the hands held fast and dragged him into the light. It was as though fire had been thrown into his essence. He could see nothing but a burning, blinding light.

"Hello, Gerald."

Eloise's voice was in his ear. Her hands were on his head, pushing and pushing. He could not see to fight back. He could not break away, even as he felt himself breaking. Even as her hands let the light into his soul. He couldn't even scream.

She had won.

OVER THE GARDEN WALL

The house wanted things to be dead. Eloise was not certain that this was the same as wanting things to die or wanting to kill things, but she was certain it preferred death to life. It was so full of death that it spread out like an aura or a stench that filled the air around it.

Eloise had noticed a long time ago that the garden was a depressing place. There was something sad and unwelcoming about it. At first, she decided it was just because no one tended it. It took care of itself. It sat beyond the house, ignored by Shane Ryan, and just existed. But there was more to it.

She went to the garden at night, and she went to the garden during the day. It was always the same. The garden was quiet, even more so than the house, which at least creaked and groaned.

The sound in the garden, what little there was, was not from the garden. The honking of a car horn carried on a breeze from a distant street. The wind howled sometimes, but that was the wind.

It was not until one day, a long time ago, when Eloise heard a raven's cry, that she realized what was wrong.

The raven sat on the garden wall. It was a small wall made of stone, and it would keep no one in or out. It was from back when the house was built, she assumed, for modern homes never had such small and useless walls. But it surely marked the edge of Shane Ryan's property, if not according to legal borders drawn up by adults who made such paperwork, then according to the will of the house.

"Where did you come from?" Eloise had asked.

The raven, of course, had no answer. But it made her realize she had never seen the bird in the garden. She had never seen any bird in the garden. Nor a rabbit, a squirrel, a rat, or a stray cat from the neighborhood. The living did not enter the yard. The house didn't want them there.

"Have you ever seen a bird here?" Eloise asked Thaddeus one day.

"What bird?" the boy replied. The two were walking by the pond the ghost of the girl had once occupied until Shane Ryan took care of her.

"Any bird."

Thaddeus thought for a long moment. Too long of a moment, and Eloise found it very trying.

"I can't remember," he said at last.

"Just say no," she told him. "There are no birds in the garden. There are no animals at all. I don't think even honey bees come to the flowers."

"I don't like bees," Thaddeus said, and Eloise sighed very audibly for him.

"Shane Ryan is the only living thing that the house likes," Eloise decided.

"It can't like him; it's a house."

"Yes, it can," Eloise said. "It hates birds and mice and bees. And if it can hate those things, it can like Shane Ryan."

"You're being silly," Thaddeus countered.

"You're being stupid because you know I'm right."

She left him then, no longer interested in wasting her time on the boy. He didn't understand at all.

Days later, Eloise found Carl in the garden, talking to Shane while he smoked a cigarette. Shane left to do some business when he was finished, but Carl remained behind.

"Is he going away again?" Eloise asked, joining the older ghost.

"For now, yes," Carl explained. Shane was very busy these days and Eloise was not sure who she envied more, Shane or the people he went to help. They must all have had such adventures beyond the house.

"Carl, do you know why the house doesn't let anything live in the garden?"

Eloise secretly knew the answer already. She wanted to know if Carl knew how much the house hated living things.

"Is this so?" he asked, and the question caught her off-guard.

"Of course it is. There are no birds here, or rabbits, or bees. Those things live in gardens, but nothing lives in ours."

Carl turned and looked across the property.

"But do you not see the Virginia creeper? The flowering quince? The forsythia? And the black-eyed Susan? There is life here."

"No," Eloise said, annoyed by Carl's answer. "Those are just plants; they don't count."

"Plants are what makes a garden a garden," he explained. She could see the barest hint of a smile on his face and knew he was teasing her. It was not funny.

"You know what I mean, Carl. Animals. The house doesn't want them to live here."

The older ghost shrugged, letting his eyes sweep across the garden and all the growth it held. He said nothing.

Eloise thought that once, it must have had a lot of living things in it. When it was new, before she was there, and before Carl and the girl in the pond and the dark ones and even Roberto. Once upon a time, when the house was brand-new and exciting and the garden was probably so full of bees and butterflies and singing birds. And then, it wasn't.

After her talk with Carl, Eloise grew accustomed to the idea that nothing would or maybe could live in the garden and did not bring it up again. So what? She thought. It could not be changed.

✶ ✶ ✶

It was autumn when she was out at the pond, escaping from Thaddeus and the others, when she saw something new stirring in the garden.

The days were growing shorter and the leaves on trees were turning the shades of winter death. Green became yellow and orange and red. Nothing was dead yet; some flowers struggled to hold on just a few days longer. But soon enough, frost would cover everything before the snow came.

There were structures in the garden, sheds for groundskeepers or landscapers or whoever maintained such a garden when the house was still bustling with life. Now, they held some supplies and nothing else, just storage for rusting old tools and pots and such. Something was moving inside one such structure.

The shed was very small, like a tiny house, with a window that faced the main house. Years of rain and wind and more had fogged the glass so that it was gray and nearly opaque, but when the light hit it just right from behind, it still passed through the front. Eloise saw a shadow moving.

It was not Shane because he was not home yet, and if he had come home, she would have known. No one else would have skipped the house and gone into the yard, and they especially would not have entered the shed and closed the door behind them.

Eloise drifted close, listening for sounds from within. She heard rustling, something scraping against wood. It sounded large.

The ghost circled the shed cautiously and then crept through the rear wall. She knew there was a shelf against the wall, something that would give her cover in case one of the dark ones had escaped the cellar.

As she pushed past the wooden walls and entered the dim space, she saw she was mistaken. It was not something from the cellar. It was a man.

He was old, older than Shane Ryan, and he wore a knit cap on his head as though winter had already come. His face was hidden behind a beard dashed with speckles of gray and wild locks of black and gray hair from under the hat. He wore a long, thick coat and gloves on his hands with the fingertips removed.

Eloise crept into the corner and watched the man as he emptied a large duffel bag of provisions. He'd already set a sleeping bag and blankets on the floor and was now pulling out a very crumpled jug of water and a can of tuna.

A handful of books were scattered on the blankets with other strange trinkets like a broken watch, a medal, some old handwritten pages, and little, painted figurines. The window that had given the man away only moments earlier was now covered by a cloth, and a tiny, camp-style stove burned dimly on the floor by the door.

"Got all that time now," the man said, and for a moment, Eloise thought he was talking to her. "Got it unpacked and rolled out."

He muttered more words that were lost in his beard and then produced a can opener for the tuna. The man settled himself and opened the can.

"Got that time, too," he told the can before drinking the liquid inside and then using a small, wide spoon to eat the contents. He placed the can in an old plastic bag when he was done.

Eloise had no doubt that this man did not have Shane's permission to be in the shed. He was an intruder, and no one liked those. Not Shane, not Carl, and not the house.

Then it occurred to Eloise that this man was in the yard. It was not that nothing could live in the yard; everything just knew not to go there. The animals had a sense of it. They knew it was dangerous. This man did not.

People were very foolish sometimes, especially the living. Eloise knew that. This man looked like he was setting up a camp, a place to stay, and that was a very bad call. She wondered if he planned to stay only the night, or if his plans were long-term. Maybe he was not a planner. He talked to himself, and his words did not make sense to her. Maybe he did not even know where he was. But he knew enough to cover the window. He knew enough to hide.

Eloise left. She thought about telling Carl but decided against it. She would keep the man her secret and see what he did.

✳ ✳ ✳

The man was still there the next day. She wondered how he would get in and out of the shed without being seen by Carl or the sisters, but she soon discovered he had pulled panels loose from the rear of the shed. He could sneak in and out and not be seen from the house. From there, he could slink down to the back of the garden and over the garden wall.

He had left his things in the shed, so Eloise knew he would be back. It took only a few hours for him to return with new items in his bag. He got cozy in his tiny home and ate another meal, this time soup that he heated on his little stove.

Eloise knew the man planned to stay. Maybe just for the winter. Maybe for as long as he could.

The state of the garden, and that of the shed, made it clear that no one spent much time in the garden. It had inadvertently signaled to the strange newcomer that he had found a safe space. But it was not safe.

✳ ✳ ✳

"How long do you think it takes the house to kill something?" Eloise asked.

She was outside with Thaddeus on the morning of the first frost. Everything glittered in the faint light from the moon in a cloudless sky like the world was covered in diamonds.

"The house doesn't kill things," Thaddeus replied.

Sometimes, Eloise did not want to talk to Thaddeus because he was very dull.

"Of course it does. It doesn't like intruders."

"That's different," the boy said.

"So... how long?"

16

"It's very quick," he answered. He was right. If someone entered the house who didn't belong there, they had little time to escape. The house moved and changed, trapping them, and making it so they could never leave.

"It is very quick," Eloise agreed.

The man had been in the shed for a few weeks at that point. The house had not killed him. But he was also on the property, not in the house. Maybe the house was not as skilled at removing things from the property. Maybe it scared away the animals but didn't kill them, and the man was not scared. Not yet, anyway.

"What if someone came here who didn't belong but didn't go in the house?" Eloise asked.

"What about it?" the boy said.

"Would the house kill them?"

"The house doesn't—"

"Oh, for God's sake. Would it try to get rid of them? Out here in the garden?"

"I don't know. You're being rude." Thaddeus left her then, and she was glad he had. Being rude was far better than being Thaddeus some days.

✳ ✳ ✳

The days grew shorter and colder, and the man stayed hidden. Shane Ryan came home, and Eloise was certain he would discover the garden intruder, but he had not. He had not even gone into the garden.

The man had made the shed more of a home. He had clothes inside and provisions stored on the shelves. There were more books and a deck of cards. She hid in the corner and listened to him sometimes as he read books. He read them out loud and also commented on them at the same time, and she found it amusing.

Eloise suspected the man was not well. He was not mad, but he was not altogether sane.

It stormed one night, and though he did a good job of staying quiet, he yelled at the thunder and the freezing rain.

"Not this time!" he raged and banged his fist on the wall. "You don't get another chance!"

She wanted to ask him what he meant, what the weather might have done to him in the past, but she did not. Instead, she waited out the early winter storm and pondered the changes in the shed.

The man had done many things to make the place his own, but something else about the shed caught Eloise's eye. The camp stove, small and always burning, was still in a place near the door, but the door was not near the stove.

She stared at the floor and then the door. The gap had widened. The floorboards were longer, she realized. The space between them was wider. And below? Darkness.

It was the house. The house knew the man was there. It was changing the shed, just as it changed the halls and rooms when it wanted to. The house could hide entire floors and create mazes within its walls. And now, it had exerted that influence in the shed.

The change was barely a change, and even the man had not noticed. Maybe the house was so far from the shed that it was hard work for it. It could only do so much so fast. But it was working, and that meant the man was in danger. The house would kill him, no matter what Thaddeus said. It would widen the floorboards until he fell through into… what?

Eloise crept down below the floor and into a space that was not meant to be there. The shed had no cellar before. It did now.

Something moved in the dark that she could not see. Eloise could see normally in any sort of darkness, and nothing was so hidden from her that she could not tell what it was. Except the dark ones in the root cellar in the house.

She moved swiftly to a wall and looked around the space. It was the cellar, the real cellar, not a space below the shed but the space below the house. It should not have existed there—could not have—but it did. The house had brought the cellar to the shed. It was there for the man.

Eloise rose from the cellar and found herself back in the house. She fled, returning to the garden and to the shed in which the man read to himself by the light of his little stove.

The house would have him soon. Maybe not that night but the next, or the night after. He would move to take a drink of water or read another book, and the space between the floorboards would swallow him up. He would tumble into the cellar, and the dark ones would have him before he had time to scream.

Eloise was angry. The man might have been an intruder, but he was harmless. He was also her secret. The house was going to take that away. Or it intended to, anyway.

She entered the shed and slapped at the fabric covering the window, knocking it down. The man looked up from his book and fell silent. He froze in place, unsure of what had happened, and then got to his knees. He reached for the window covering and Eloise leaned close to his camp stove. She exhaled, and the flame flickered and then died out. The shed fell to darkness.

"No, you don't," the man said.

"Yes. I do," Eloise replied. It was just a whisper in the dark and the man gasped. Eloise stood in the corner and watched him as the fear took hold like the cold from outside had turned him into a statue. He didn't move, and he barely breathed. He needed encouragement.

Hands on the walls, Eloise drummed her fists. The shed shook, the walls rattled, and things fell from the shelves.

The man cried out and grabbed his bag, running for the loose boards. He passed through Eloise and cried out again as a wave of cold overcame him.

She watched him go to the far end of the yard and over the garden wall. Like the raven, he did not return.

Nonetheless, she was glad he'd showed up to visit.

Coming Home

The family picnicking in the park made Eloise angry, but she wasn't sure why. Maybe it was the little girl in her pretty pink dress with bows in her hair, snacking on cookies and juice without a care in the world. Maybe it was the way the mother and father talked while looking at their phones. They ignored the girl as she ran and chased butterflies, and collected tiny, purple wildflowers. Something about them just rubbed her the wrong way.

Eloise rarely went to the park during the day. She rarely went anywhere when the sun was still out. The world felt wrong to her in the light. The darkness was comforting because it was natural. Light was a thing; darkness was the absence of it, and that made her feel welcome and at home.

Still, the park was a place she had to visit in the daytime if she wanted to visit at all. Few people went to the park at night, so it was very uninteresting. There was a playground there, and a fountain and benches. Eloise knew those things had to be used during the day, and so she went to see for herself.

The park was the only such place she could reach from the house. There were some fields and other homes near where Shane Ryan lived, but only one park. That made it special.

"Bekka, don't run too far," the mother said loudly, not looking to see where Bekka was.

The little girl was standing on a footpath a short distance from her parents. She had stopped at a bench where an old woman sat, and the two were talking. Eloise was in the shadow of a maple tree and not close enough to hear the conversation, but the older woman was very animated and doing most of the talking.

Old people were very fascinating to Eloise. To have lived for such a long time was unusual, she thought. Someone like Shane Ryan seemed old to her because even though she was born before him, he had lived much longer. This woman was far older than even Shane. She had avoided death well.

"Bekka!" the mother yelled again. She put down her phone and looked around, finally catching sight of the little girl a few yards away, speaking to the old woman.

The girl ignored her mother, and so did the woman. The mother said something to the father, who looked over at the child and seemed unmoved. The mother spoke to him angrily, got to her feet, and strode quickly to the girl, taking her by the hand.

Eloise moved closer. The mother nearly dragged Bekka back to their picnic spot with a tight grip on the girl's small hand.

"We don't talk to strangers. How many times have I told you that?" the mother scolded.

"I was just talking to a lady," the little girl protested.

"It doesn't matter," her mother cut her off. "A lady can be just as dangerous as a man. All strangers can be dangerous."

Eloise had learned that the people you know can be far more dangerous than strangers, but that point would probably have been lost on the mother. She was not the sort of person who listened well.

"Don't argue with your mother," the father said. He did not look up from his phone.

"Thanks for the help," the mother said, her tone suggesting that she did not mean it.

Eloise looked back at the older woman. She wore a large fur coat that seemed like it was not suited to the weather given how everyone else was dressed. She had on more jewelry than Eloise had ever seen on another person.

Eventually, the family finished the picnic and packed their things. Eloise watched them go and decided she never wanted to see them again. Once they left the park, she made her way along the shadow of a tree, pretending it was a balance beam, and walked closer to the lady on the bench.

"Oh, aren't you darling?" the woman said.

Eloise stopped, her hands out dramatically as though keeping her balance for real, and looked at the woman. Her eyes were a muddy green, and her smile made her wrinkled face that much more wrinkled. She was speaking to Eloise.

"Thank you," she replied.

"Such a pretty dress," the lady added.

Eloise looked at her gray and tattered dress, caught in the lifeless state it had been when she died, and said nothing.

"I came here with my Darla," the woman continued. "She loves the park so much."

"Is that your daughter?" Eloise asked.

"Oh yes, my darling Darla. She loves the park so much."

Eloise looked around but did not see any other little girls. She approached the lady and then sat down on the bench next to her, only slightly nervous that someone else could see her.

"Do you like the swings, dear?" the old lady asked.

Eloise looked over her shoulder at the swing set behind them.

"I like swings. They're fun," she admitted.

The old woman beamed and pulled a large leather purse from her side. She undid a metal clasp and began rummaging through piles of crumpled paper and other odd items.

"I have some candies in here. Would you like a candy?" she asked.

"No, thank you," Eloise replied. She did want a candy, but there was nothing she could do with one if she had it, so there was no real need for it.

The woman found one for herself, a small treat wrapped in gold cellophane, and popped it into her mouth.

"My Darla loves the park," she said again. "What's your name, dear?"

"Eloise," the ghost replied.

"Eloise!" the woman exclaimed, her voice higher and her expression delighted. "I had an Aunt Eloise! I haven't seen her in so long."

"Is Darla here?" Eloise asked, looking around the park again. There were fewer people than when she'd arrived, and aside from two older boys, no children were playing in the park.

"You know Darla?"

Eloise did not think that Darla was in the park. The old lady was likely confused. It made her lose interest. Maybe she would come back another day to meet the girl.

"Okay, well, have a nice day," Eloise said as she got off the bench.

The old woman smiled at her and searched through her purse again.

"Would you like a candy, dear?" she asked.

"No, thank you," Eloise replied slowly.

She left the woman then. She was very forgetful, it seemed, and Eloise was not keen to talk to someone who kept forgetting what they were talking about.

It was a long while before Eloise returned to the park. She had thought of the old woman again and returned to see if her daughter was with her.

The weather was cooler, and there were no picnickers when Eloise arrived, but she found the old woman on the bench once more. She wore the same coat and the same jewelry. She carried the same purse.

"Is Darla here today?" Eloise asked as she approached the woman.

"Look at you; how precious," the woman answered. "What's your name, dear?"

"I'm Eloise. Like your aunt," she explained.

"Like… Aunt Eloise," the woman said, more to herself than the ghost.

"Is Darla here?"

"Oh. Darla? No, she's not… she must be at home, then. Don't you think?"

"Maybe," Eloise agreed.

The woman seemed sad now, not the joyful, albeit confused person from their last encounter.

"Should we go home, then?" she asked. If her daughter was home, it made sense for the old woman to be home as well.

"If you like," Eloise replied.

The old woman took a moment to collect her things and make sure she had everything. She walked slowly toward the northern park exit, heading in the direction of Berkley Street.

"I didn't know Aunt Eloise was coming to visit," the woman mumbled after several steps. Eloise had not joined the woman, but as she heard her talking, she moved to catch up, walking alongside her.

"I think I'll make us tea," the woman said as she turned down the walkway to a house that could have easily been swapped for Shane Ryan's.

It was not the same house, but it had the same air about it. It was large and covered in spikes and peaks and windows like a palace. But unlike the house on Berkley Street, this one had been painted sky blue. Though much of the paint was peeling now, and the garden was overgrown, it was full of buzzing bees and chirping insects and looked very warm and full of life.

Eloise followed the woman into her home. She waited as the woman removed her shoes and hung up her purse and large coat. The interior of her home was dark, and there were many piles of things in many places. She had books stacked in hallways and newspapers stacked on tables. There were clothes on chairs and boxes behind those same chairs.

She led them to the kitchen, where there were bags, cans, boxes, and bins as far as the eye could see. It looked as though the woman had never thrown out a piece of trash.

The refuse piles didn't faze the woman. She pushed things aside to fill a kettle with water and set it on the gas stove. Eloise swept her hand near the flame, disturbing the air and knocking a pile of boxes to the floor before they caught fire.

"We have to get ready for Aunt Eloise's visit, dear," the woman said, putting two mugs on the counter as she turned to look at the ghost. "Gracious, look at the state of you. Your dress is all gray and dirty. Come, let's get you cleaned up."

The woman made her way out of the kitchen and down the hall toward a staircase. Eloise followed, not sure what was happening but still curious. They made their way to the second floor and then up to a third floor on stairs with a missing handrail. Then the woman paused, breathing heavily, as she turned to look at one final staircase.

Shane's home did not have four floors, at least not all the time. The fourth floor in his house was a ghost floor that came and went as the house desired. But this was very real, and the journey was taxing on the older woman, who was still breathing with difficulty.

"We don't have to go up," Eloise offered.

"Nonsense, love," the woman replied. "The state of you! We must get you dolled up for Aunt Eloise. We'll find your pretty yellow dress."

The woman resumed her climb, and Eloise followed. The house was a dismal thing this far up. Cobwebs hung thick from corners and the dust on both the stairs and landing made it clear no one had gone to the fourth floor in a long while, possibly years. She wondered why there might be a dress up there but did not ask.

The clutter on the upper floor was so much worse than it was below. Stacks of boxes and trash were piled to the ceiling in places. The path through was narrow at best, and the woman had difficulty navigating it. She led them to a room midway down the hall and paused at the door.

"Yes, we'll find your dress, won't we, darling," she said, more to herself than Eloise. She looked at the ghost, but her eyes seemed distant.

26

She smiled and reached out but did not touch her.

"You were always so beautiful in that dress."

The door opened, and Eloise said nothing. Dust rose in motes all around them, and the air was so thick with it that it looked like a fog. The curtains were drawn, and the room was dark, but Eloise could see everything.

It had been a girl's room once. There was a vanity covered in boxes and small baubles. There was makeup and brushes and ribbons and clips for hair. All of it was lost to the grime of old age.

A dresser, once white trimmed in blue, was now gray and faded like Eloise's dress, and it was hard to tell what color the carpet had once been.

Eloise was surprised to see that the room was not a mess otherwise. There were no stacks of boxes or piles of rubbish. It was just unused, it seemed. Forgotten.

There was a bed on the wall to the left of the door, and it was as large a bed as Eloise had ever seen. Four columns rose, one from each corner, and were connected by sheaves of a muslin fabric that was encased in dusty old cobwebs.

The fabric hung between the posters like curtains, offering privacy to whoever might have used the bed long ago when the room was still lived in.

"I kept it the way you left it," the old woman said. "I knew you'd want it the same when you came back."

"Came back?" Eloise asked.

"Of course, darling. I knew you'd come back. I told them you just left for school. I told everyone. I knew you'd come home."

The woman made her way to the dresser and struggled to open a drawer. She searched through clothing, and Eloise's eyes were drawn back to the bed.

"Who did you tell?" she asked.

"I had to tell them something," the woman said. "The police came by twice, and your friend Mary Elizabeth. They kept asking so many questions, so I told them you left for school."

Eloise approached the bed. Her eyes worked well in the dark, and she could see something on the bed through the material that kept it obscured. The old woman rifled through drawers and Eloise walked through the cobwebs and fabric and looked down at the bed.

The body had been there a very long time. The bedding was stained beneath the dust and darkened by the rot. The flesh was old and dry now, barely more than paper stretched thin over bone.

She was not a child, not a young one of Eloise's age. None of the things in the room looked like they were for a child, either. A young woman, perhaps. From many years ago. Decades.

"Did the police not look here?" Eloise asked.

"Oh, no. I took them to the other room downstairs. Your old room, darling. And they read your journal and looked at your things. A man came and told me you never registered at the school. That you must have run away. But I knew you'd be back."

"She—" Eloise began, leaving the bedside. "I didn't run away."

The woman turned and looked at her once more.

"I tried to help, but it was so fast. The handrail was always so loose, wasn't it? Even when we moved in, it was loose. I never thought…"

Eloise remembered that the handrail on the third-floor stairway was missing. It left the stairs open. Down to the second floor, and then down to the first. A straight drop if someone were to slip.

"It was an accident," Eloise said.

The old woman shook her head, raising a hand to her mouth.

"I never thought it was dangerous. I meant to fix it," she said, choking on the words. She broke down then, sobbing and gasping as she stared at the little girl.

She should have told the police, Eloise thought. It was just an accident. But as she watched the woman collapse to her knees, her face buried in her hands, she wondered how true that was.

In her mind, it was not an accident. Maybe that was not something she could face. Maybe that was why she thought Eloise, who was too young to be her child and could not have looked like her, was her daughter now. Maybe she needed to convince herself that things were different than they were.

Deep in the house, a high-pitched sound erupted. The kettle in the kitchen had reached a boil and was screaming. Eloise approached the woman and knelt at her side.

"I'm so sorry," the woman sobbed. "I'm so sorry."

Eloise reached out and touched the woman's back, the cold of her hand just barely reaching her.

"It's okay. I came back," she said.

The woman looked up, her face damp as more tears fell.

"You did, my love. You came home."

"I did," Eloise agreed. "Why don't we go back down and have tea, and you can tell me more about Aunt Eloise?"

The old woman sniffed and nodded slowly. She got back to her feet, all dusty and disheveled.

"Yes. You're so cold, love. Let's get you a cup of tea."

She led the way from the room, with the ghost just a step behind.

Eloise looked back at the bed for only a moment before leaving.

THE GIRL WHO WASN'T THERE

Katy Price had never had an invisible friend, and she was not happy that her very first one looked like a dead person. She did not know what everyone else's invisible friends looked like, however, and that meant she didn't know if hers was strange or not.

Eloise had ribbons in her hair and wore a frilly dress that was probably once white but was now very dirty. Her skin was pale and dull, and she was very skinny. Her teeth were yellow, and sometimes Katy caught her staring with a look in her eyes that sent a shiver down her spine and made the hair on her arms stand on end. But then Eloise would say that everything was fine, and they would play a fun game, and everything was okay again.

Katy met Eloise in the backyard just after Katy's sixth birthday. Katy's family had just moved to Nashua, and she did not have any friends yet besides a little dog named Jasper who lived at the end of the street. She was very sad that her birthday party had just been with her mom and dad and her hamster, Fidget.

She was playing on the small trampoline her dad had bought when she saw the strange little girl just standing there, watching. She had not come in through the gate and she had not jumped over the fence, so Katy was not sure how the girl got into their yard.

"Do you live around here?" Katy asked.

"I live in a house on Berkley Street," the girl replied.

"I don't know where that is."

Katy had not stopped bouncing on her trampoline, and the skinny girl pointed into the distance.

"Over there."

Katy stopped and got off the trampoline.

"My name is Katy, and I just turned six," she said.

"My name is Eloise. I'm a little bit older than you... ummmm, but I'm also way older than you."

Katy cocked her head to one side and looked confused for a moment before she went on.

"Do you want to play?"

Eloise looked at Katy and seemed hesitant but then nodded.

"Yes! What can we play?"

Katy's parents had bought her an entire backyard playset when they moved in, with a slide and swings and a little wooden castle that even had a tower with a flag and binoculars that let her see everything very close.

"We could play in my castle," she suggested.

Eloise looked at the wooden structure and agreed.

Katy was the first to climb the ladder at the back of her castle, and when she got to the top, Eloise was already sitting inside.

"How did you do that?" Katy asked, looking down at where she had left the mysterious little girl only a moment earlier.

"How did I do what?"

"How did you get here before me?"

"I can go anywhere I want," Eloise explained, "but usually I stay at home."

"Can you go to Disneyland?" Katy asked, hoping her new friend could take her.

"No. I mean, I can go anywhere, but only close to home."

"Oh. How come?"

Eloise shrugged as Katy climbed into the small space. It was very cold despite it being warm outside, and she pulled her knees up tightly in front of herself and hugged them.

"Do you go to school?" Katy asked.

"No."

"Why not?"

"Don't need to," Eloise replied. She was looking at Katy's toys around them, but she did not touch anything.

"Everyone needs to go to school," Katy told her. Her parents had told her that, and she knew it was true.

"Not me."

"Don't your parents make you go?"

"I don't have parents. I have Shane Ryan, but he's not my dad, and he doesn't make me do anything. Except sometimes he tells me to make less noise or to play somewhere else, but never in the cellar."

"Is he your uncle?"

"No," Eloise answered.

Eloise was not good at answering questions, Katy realized. She wondered what sort of place Eloise might live in, given how skinny and dirty she was. If she didn't have parents, maybe no one was taking care of her.

"Do you want to have dinner with us? My mom is making spaghetti," Katy offered.

"Sure," Eloise said, and Katy was thrilled.

✳ ✳ ✳

"Mom, can my new friend Eloise stay for dinner?"

Jessica Price turned away from the simmering pot on the stove and looked down at her daughter. She was alone and dirty, but that was no surprise.

"Eloise?" she asked with a smile.

"Yes. She lives nearby, and she came to the yard to play, and I asked her if she would like some of your spaghetti."

"Oh, well, sure. It's nice that you've met a playmate."

Katy looked to her left and then up at her mother. A silence lingered

33

and Jessica stirred her sauce.

"Is everything alright?"

"Didn't you hear Eloise? She said she's never had spaghetti."

"Oh. I didn't hear her, no," Jessica answered and realized what was happening.

She had hoped Katy would make new friends in the neighborhood, but that was probably more likely to happen once school started. An imaginary friend was not something she'd expected, but she'd read it was pretty normal. Jessica had an imaginary friend named Buggins when she was a child, so she couldn't find Eloise all that unusual.

"Well, she can have as much as she wants, and I hope she likes it. But first, you both need to wash up."

Katy looked to her left again and then turned away, heading from the kitchen to the washroom. A gust of cold air rushed past Jessica as her daughter walked by, and she shuddered, absently reminding herself to check the setting on the air conditioner when she had a moment.

✱ ✱ ✱

The water rushed from the faucet and Katy thrust her hands in, sloshing them around with a squirt of soap from the pump on the counter.

"My mom says if you don't wash your hands, you can get sick," Katy said, letting Eloise have the spot in front of the sink.

"I don't need to wash my hands," her friend replied.

"But we were playing in the yard, and the yard is dirty."

"I don't get dirty."

Katy frowned and glanced at the other girl's dress. She did not want to be rude, but if Eloise did not think she was dirty, then she was mistaken.

"You should do it, anyway. So Mom wouldn't scold us," Katy suggested.

"I can't," Eloise answered.

34

"It's easy!"

She reached for Eloise's hand. Her fingertips passed through the other girl's flesh like it was nothing. But it wasn't nothing; it was cold like slipping her hand into the freezer.

Katy gasped. Her arm was extended, and she could see where it had vanished inside of the other girl like it had become a part of her. She pulled back quickly, afraid that somehow her hand had disappeared forever, and it reappeared, the same as always only covered in gooseflesh from the chill.

"See?" Eloise said. She put her hands under the faucet and the water flowed right through them. "I don't need to wash."

"Are you… a ghost?" Katy asked.

"Yes," Eloise answered.

"Does that mean you're dead?"

Eloise nodded and Katy reached out to touch her again. The ghost's expression became very mischievous, and she intercepted Katy's hand with her own. Their fingers touched, but the cold was so much colder this time. Katy yipped and pulled her finger back, the tip red from the sudden freeze. After the initial shock, she giggled and so did Eloise.

"How do you do that?" she asked.

"I just do," the ghost explained. "It's very cold when you die."

"I'm sorry you died. Did it hurt?"

"Yes," Eloise answered. "I don't want to talk about that. Let's go have spaghetti."

"Can you eat it?"

"No, but you can tell me about it."

They ran from the bathroom together, giggling as Eloise gave Katy another quick, cold zap.

✳ ✳ ✳

Eloise did not tell Shane Ryan about Katy. She did not tell anyone because Katy was her friend and no one else's. She did not want Thaddeus or the girl Frank had brought with him named Princess trying to steal her away.

They did not play every day, only some days, when Eloise remembered to visit. Sometimes, she forgot to visit for a week or more, but Katy never seemed to mind. She did so more often when Shane was not home because it was more boring in the house without him around.

She had missed Katy's seventh birthday but when her eighth birthday came around, Eloise remembered and showed up on time for her party, which included a barbecue and cake and ice cream. Eloise had none of those things and that was okay, but there were many other little boys and girls around them, and that bothered her.

Katy had been in school for two years and made many friends, and they all came to the party. There were at least twelve of them in the backyard, and they brought presents wrapped in ribbons and colorful paper and stacked them all on a table. None of them saw Eloise and none of them spoke to her.

"We should play in your castle," Eloise said to Katy when she was eating a hot dog. Her friend ignored her while another girl named Jasmine told Katy about her new video game.

"We should go play," Eloise said again.

Katy looked at her sideways and was about to answer when someone else started talking and she focused on them instead. Eloise knew what she was doing. Sometimes Shane did it. Not everyone could see ghosts, so when others were present, they ignored her.

An older man with a little dog came up to Katy and handed her a present. She thanked him and bent down to pet his dog. She called the dog Jasper, but Jasper's eyes were locked on Eloise, and he ignored the living girl.

Eloise hissed and Jasper jumped. The dog barked and gnashed his teeth and bit Katy's hand hard. The teeth sunk deep and drew blood. Katy screamed and Jasmine screamed, and other children screamed, too.

The old man apologized. Katy's parents rushed to her, and her dad asked the man to leave. The man apologized and said Katy could come and play with Jasper any time and that the dog was sorry, too. Now everyone was talking and ignoring Eloise. She had not meant to get her friend hurt; it was an accident.

"Why did you do that?" Katy yelled, clutching her bleeding hand, and looking back at Eloise. Everyone else was still talking. No one looked at Eloise except Katy. It was the only thing she had said to her all day.

"It was an accident. I'm sorry," Eloise said.

Katy shook her head, tears streaming down her face as her mother held a pile of napkins to her bloody hand and lifted the girl to carry into the house.

"You're not my friend," Katy shouted as she was whisked away.

Eloise scowled at the door as it closed behind them. Other parents and children spoke in a frenzy, left behind in the aftermath. The man and his dog stood at the gate to the yard. He was talking to Katy's father, still apologizing for what happened.

It was his fault, not Eloise's. He brought the dog. He was the reason she was bitten.

Eloise locked eyes with the dog, and he growled. Someone asked the old man to leave again, and he did. Katy was still crying inside the house. Nobody noticed when Eloise left to follow the man.

He took his dog, muttering quietly to the animal about being good to little kids. Eloise followed, sticking to the shadows to not alarm the dog any more than she had.

She went yard to yard, tree to tree, following until the old man came to a big, old house at the end of the street. It was not as big as her house on Berkley Street, but it was still larger than most, and hard to see from the street behind all the bushes and trees.

The old man walked his dog up the path to the door and slipped inside. Eloise followed him.

The man's house was dark inside. He kept his curtains drawn and used only dim lights in some rooms. The living room was full of old furniture and framed photos. The dining room was the same.

The dog went to the kitchen and drank water from a bowl while the man puttered about, mumbling and fidgeting with the thermostat, and then hanging up a sweater and straightening some pictures.

She left him, wandering through the rest of the house. There were four bedrooms but three were untouched and a little dusty like they had not been used in a long time. One still had an unmade bed and a half-eaten sandwich on the nightstand. It was the only one with a television.

There was only one toothbrush in the bathroom, and Eloise decided he lived alone. She made her way to the basement. He kept boxes down there, so many boxes, all with neat labels. Blankets. Kitchenware. Photo albums. There were lots of photo albums.

The basement looked small at first, but Eloise discovered there were other rooms, which were hidden. There was a door behind a bookshelf. She passed through it and into a red-lit room for making photographs. It had bottles of chemicals and trays and equipment. Some pictures hung from strings; others were stacked in little piles. Pictures of houses, and cars, of people she'd noticed at the party, and other people Eloise had never seen. There were pictures of Katy and other girls. Eloise frowned.

She noticed another door leading into another room. This one was sparse and small and had no windows. There was a dirty rug on the floor, and the mattress had no blankets. It had not been used in a long time, she thought, and it was much uglier than the upstairs rooms.

"Who are you?"

Eloise was surprised by the voice. She turned swiftly and watched as a little girl peered out at her from beneath the rickety metal bed frame. She was younger than Eloise. Or she had been when she became a ghost.

"My name is Eloise. Who are you?"

"Ashley," the other ghost answered. "You have to go."

"No, I don't," Eloise said.

"Yes, you do! If he catches you, he'll lock you in. The door only opens from outside and you'll never, ever get out."

She pointed a frail, white hand at the door, and Eloise looked. There was no doorknob, just a keyhole.

"I can get out," Eloise explained. She walked to the door, then through it, then back into the room.

Ashley gasped.

"You can do it, too," Eloise assured her.

Ashley shook her head and Eloise crouched to get a better look at her.

"Why are you under there?"

"He can't see me here. Hasn't seen me in a long time," she explained.

Eloise wondered how long it had been. Not so long, she didn't think. Not as long as Eloise had been dead.

"Did he kill you?" she asked.

"What?" Ashley replied, her voice a shaky whisper. "What do you mean?"

Eloise realized the other girl did not know she was dead.

"How long have you been hiding here?"

"I don't know," the girl answered.

Eloise stood up again. The man had hurt Ashley, and he had hurt Katy, too. It was his fault. He was the bad one, not Eloise.

"Do you want to leave? There's a birthday party we could visit, and they have a castle we can play in."

"I can't," Ashley replied. "I can't ever leave."

"I can. And you can come with me."

Ashley shook her head.

"He'll come after us."

Eloise sighed. He would not, but Ashley didn't understand that. She would have to make her understand.

She left and returned to the red room. It was not always easy for her to move things, but she did so now. She smashed the trays of chemicals against the walls and the door. She slammed the tables and the ceiling and made as much noise as she could until she heard footsteps above. And then she waited.

The man came downstairs and moved the bookcase aside. He entered the red room and cursed when he saw the terrible mess. He did not see Eloise, and she said nothing while he tried to understand what could have happened. She left him there and backed into the room with Ashley. She stood at the door and raised her hand.

Knock. Knock. Knock.

"Who's there?" the man asked from the other room, confused and scared now.

Eloise waited at the door until she heard footsteps and then metal scraping metal. Tumblers turning. Click and roll and ca-chunk.

The door opened.

Ashley scampered back to the darkest shadow beneath the bed, but Eloise stayed where she was. The man flicked on a switch, and a single bulb hummed to life above their heads. The shadows vanished and Ashley was exposed, but the man could not see her any more than he saw Eloise.

His breathing was rapid, and sweat had just begun to bead around the edges of his hairline. His eyes were wide, and he stared around the room in a panic, looking for what he would never see.

He turned on his heels, and Eloise slammed a fist as hard as she could into his gut. He crumpled to the floor, caught off-guard, the wind knocked from his body.

"Get out of here," she ordered the other girl.

Ashley's fear of moving was not as strong as her fear of being disobedient. She scuttled out from under the bed and ran past the man. Eloise took her hand and pulled her into the red room.

"What…?" the man said.

He had left the key in the door. Eloise looked at the bulb on the ceiling. The temperature dropped, and the glass shattered, plunging the man into darkness as the door pulled shut.

"No!" came a muffled, nearly imperceptible yell from the other side of the door. The walls stopped the sound. They kept the screams inside.

She pulled the key from the door, dropped it on the floor, and then turned to the other girl.

"Do you want to play?" she asked.

THINGS SEEN

Eloise watched the dead bird under a tree as it rotted. The process was very slow. For a couple of days, the bird looked just fine. Then, after the ants and other bugs got to it, its feathers became unruly and dirty. Its eyes became crusty and dark, and the body looked like it had shriveled. She wondered if it smelled rotten, but she had no way to tell.

The feathers created a kind of husk over the body, and it made it hard for her to tell just how decayed the flesh was on the inside. Was it moist, she wondered? Were there things inside, swirling in the bird's guts, and eating the rotten organs? She did not know.

In time, the bird was little more than a pile of feathers stuck to dried, brown bones. Something had come one day and taken away most of the body. The skull was gone, along with the ribs. She wondered who might do such a thing. A cat, she decided. Or a very strange child.

She found the dead bird at the back of a home close to Shane Ryan's house. The homeowners had allowed their yard to grow unruly. It differed from the yard at Shane's house, which was kept immaculate even when he didn't do anything about it. The house itself made sure everything was neat.

Eloise liked the other yard better. Things lived there, like rabbits and squirrels and mice. And, for a time, that bird.

When she could sneak away at night, she went into the neighborhood and watched how other people lived their lives. Their homes were so bright, full of lights and electronics and people and noises. It was so different from what she was used to.

No one knew she visited the homes. Not Carl, not the sisters, and certainly not Shane. He would be against it, she was certain. None of them would approve of her playing tricks on people, even though they were all harmless. She made sure no one got hurt badly because she was responsible like that.

She stood in kitchens, hidden in the corners, and watched parents make meals for their children. Or families sitting on couches in front of televisions, laughing and staring for hours on end. Their whole lives were in their lit-up homes.

She did the same at the house with the dead bird in the yard. She crept through the halls and watched the people who lived there. A man in a suit was the father, and he wore his suit all week long and worked until after dark every day.

The man had a wife, and she worked too, but only during the day. She cooked and cleaned. They had a teenage son, and he was in his room all the time. They barely spoke to each other, and Eloise could see they were all very miserable.

So she tried to help by moving things around their house every night. Sometimes, she took the father's keys and put them in drawers. Sometimes, she took the mother's pills from a medicine cabinet in the bathroom. She hid the remote controls for TVs or the boy's video games. She put money under the sofas. She broke eggs in the refrigerator. Eloise had hoped they would talk to each other and figure it out, but they never did. Every day, they only blamed each other.

In another house, a woman lived alone with five cats. The cats could see Eloise, and they did not like her. So sometimes, she ran through the house and made them all dash away in every direction.

Some houses were boring one day and exciting the next. There was no way to predict it, so she often went home to home when she had the time, looking in quickly to see what was happening before moving on. There were almost a dozen homes she felt were her favorites.

One of them was a house on the corner where a woman named Jasmine lived. Eloise liked her very much. Jasmine was young and beautiful, and Eloise pretended that maybe she would have been like Jasmine if she had grown up.

Jasmine had long, beautiful hair, and she sang to herself when she thought she was alone. She smiled when she talked to people on her telephone, and she kept her house spotless.

Then, Jasmine began a relationship with a man named Taylor, and he was always at Jasmine's house now. Eloise didn't like Taylor. He was smug, and she did not care for smugness. He sometimes called Jasmine stupid when she said things. He laughed when he said it, and she laughed, too. Eloise got angry because it wasn't funny at all.

At first, Taylor and Jasmine always laughed, until it became less and less often. Sometimes, they yelled at each other. She would be alone and Taylor arrived late, and they argued about why he came home so late or how he smelled.

Sometimes, Taylor was angry when Jasmine went out with friends. She often went out on weekends with other women who showed up to get her, and Eloise envied them all. Jasmine had so many friends who were always dressed up and very pretty. She wished she could be one of them. Wherever they went, it was always too far for her to follow.

Taylor waited for Jasmine some nights and when she got home, he'd ask her where she had been, and who she had been with. They would fight and yell, and he would leave, and she would cry.

While Eloise watched the rotting bird, she realized it would be nice to kill Taylor. He was a bad person and Jasmine was good. It would be easy to kill him. He didn't even need to be in the house. She could lure him into the yard and kill him by the apple tree that grew there. He could rot into the ground like the little bird and make the apples grow plump and delicious.

But Eloise knew she could not kill Taylor. She knew it was wrong to kill him, and that Shane would be mad if she did. She remembered how upset he had gotten when she had killed that cop. And when she had blinded Victor.

It was nice to fantasize about killing Taylor, though.

When Taylor called Jasmine names, Eloise thought about pulling his tongue from his mouth and choking him with it. When he yelled at his girlfriend, Eloise thought about pushing his head under the water in a tub to see how long he could stay there.

It was not fun to visit Jasmine with Taylor around because Eloise couldn't stop thinking of killing him. So Eloise spent more time playing jokes on the angry family or trying to get the cat lady's cats to run where she wanted them to run. It made her less angry to not hear so much yelling.

$$* * *$$

Eloise did not know what day it was when she drifted past Jasmine's house again. It was very late, though. The sun had set many hours earlier and was probably close to rising again. The neighborhood was silent, and it was close to the time when she normally headed home. Once everyone was asleep, it was not much fun to spend time there.

She had stopped at the house because she heard a sound, and it made her more curious.

As soon as Eloise entered, something rushed toward her. She had come through the back into the kitchen. Almost instantly, a body rushed through her. There was a brief pause as whoever it had been gasped, the cold of Eloise's ghostly form enveloping them unexpectedly. But then, the person opened the back door and fled.

She turned and saw only a dark figure in a hooded sweatshirt running past the apple tree and toward the fence. They climbed quickly and vanished beyond into the night. Eloise let them go, more concerned with what such a person might have been doing in Jasmine's house at such an hour.

Room to room she drifted, from kitchen to dining room to bathroom and beyond. On the main floor, nothing looked out of place or unusual at all. There were subtle changes—new pillows, a new chair—that had happened since her last visit, but nothing to make a stranger burst out the door in such a hurry.

Eloise headed upstairs. She passed through the ceiling and then the floor of the second story. Her eyes scanned every dark corner and discovered little of interest until she reached the bedroom.

She had gone into Jasmine's bedroom before. She had caught her there asleep once when she first began to visit, and it made her feel uncomfortable. To watch someone alive, sleeping and defenseless, made her feel somehow more aware of how different she was as a ghost. As something dead. She liked to watch people live their lives, not lie in a bed unaware of life itself.

Things were different this time. Jasmine was there but not lying peacefully at rest. One arm hung over the edge of her disheveled bed. Her hair was splayed out on the mattress, half covered by the sheet that had been pulled up. Her eyes were open and staring sightlessly at the ceiling.

Eloise hovered over her. The woman's eyes were damp, moisture from tears still glistening on the sides of her face in the faint light that came through the window. Her lips were parted, as though caught in a gasp, and her chest was still and silent. It did not take long to realize she was not breathing.

There was a wound on the side of Jasmine's head. Blood had caked in her hair, and Eloise could see it had stained the mattress below. Her neck was red and bruised. Something had put a lot of pressure on it. Eloise knew she had been choked. To death, maybe, if the wound on her head had not done it.

The person who had run through Eloise had killed Jasmine. It had to have been Taylor. It was what made sense.

Eloise did not know where Taylor lived or if it was even close enough for her to find. But she needed to do something. So she left the house quickly, angrily, and moved through the yard and past the fence. Too much time had passed. Taylor had escaped, and there was no sign of the direction he had gone. He could have been anywhere.

She returned to the house and her friend. She was not a friend like Shane Ryan, but Jasmine was still something. She would have been a friend. Of that, Eloise was certain. In another place and in another time, she and Jasmine would have gotten along very well.

Eloise waited as long as she dared but no one came for Jasmine. The ghost returned home, slinking through shadows until she reached her house on Berkley Street and hid away from the others while the daylight hours passed.

By sundown, she was gone again.

✳ ✳ ✳

Jasmine's house was silent and empty. Eloise returned to the bedroom and found the woman's body still there. The blood in her hair had dried almost black, and her eyes had become foggy. Her flesh was paler now. No one had found her.

Eloise sat on the bed and waited. Cars passed outside, and she looked to see if they belonged to people coming to help. None of them did. She left again by dawn.

There were flies in the room the next night, but still, no one had come for Jasmine. Eloise stared into the milky eyes, wondering what they had seen. Had Taylor been angry about her spending time with her friends again? Or talking too loud on her phone?

Eloise was angry that she had not been there. If she had been there, she could have done something. Shane Ryan would have understood. If she intervened, it would have been okay. It would have been a good thing. She could have saved Jasmine's life, and the woman would still be—

Then a window cracked, the sound of crunching glass surprising

Eloise, and she looked at it. Frost rimmed the edges, and she realized the room had grown colder. Her anger had pulled the cold from the darkness and frozen the room. She looked at Jasmine's body and whispered a quiet apology for ruining the woman's private space.

* * *

When Eloise returned the next day, the house was different. There was police tape outside and things had been moved, though she could not pinpoint everything that was different. Her focus was only on the bed. Jasmine was gone. Someone had come for her at last.

Eloise sat down again and wondered where they had taken her friend. Somewhere to clean her up, Eloise hoped, to make her beautiful again, and then get her ready. Someone would take her to a cemetery, and she would go inside a pretty box, and they would bury her forever. That was what happened to dead people. Most dead people.

Someone would find Taylor. The police would find him because of what he did, and they would put him in prison forever. Or maybe even kill him. Eloise was not sure if that was a thing that they could do, but it was what should happen.

Eloise had never looked at someone in a grave. She wondered if Jasmine would be like the bird. Would she look the same for a very long time and then slowly get dirty and thin? Would she wither to bones and dried meat like Eloise had once done? Maybe it had to happen to everyone, even if they found you in time and put you in a pretty box.

The house changed many times in the days that followed. Someone came to take Jasmine's belongings. Eventually, everything was gone and then replaced with not just new things, but new people. A new family moved in, and they were not as pretty or interesting as Jasmine, so Eloise stayed away from them.

She didn't avoid the house, she just didn't return. Not often, anyway.

And rarely inside. She stood outside and looked at it sometimes, looking at the window she had cracked that the new family had replaced.

It was on a night like that when a car drove up slowly and stopped.

Normally, Eloise paid cars no mind. They were loud and fast and never interesting to her. But this car was slow, and when it stopped, she looked at it for just a moment. Just long enough to see Taylor.

He sat in the driver's seat and stared at the house. The look on his face was wistful, sad even, and Eloise could see tears forming in the corners of his eyes. Maybe she had misjudged him. He was feeling Jasmine's loss, too. Maybe her death was random, a burglar or a crazed killer who had targeted her.

She watched him watch the house and her eyes took in the details: the curve of his lips as they quivered, the way his nose scrunched when he sniffled. Then she focused on the dark knit of the sweater he wore, and the hood bunched behind him against the headrest.

There was nothing very unique about the sweater. A hundred people probably had ones just like it. Even Shane had a few just like it. But Eloise knew this one. She had felt it. It had passed right through her. She could identify every stitch.

She did not know why no one had punished Taylor for what he had done. Maybe he was still on the run. Maybe he had tricked the police, and they did not know he was the one they were after. It didn't matter. He had murdered Jasmine.

And he was right there.

She was in the car in a heartbeat, staring at the man only inches from his face. She watched his breath appear in a cloud of mist as he reached for a knob in the car.

"What the hell?" he whispered to himself.

Eloise leaned in so close that she was almost touching him.

"Hell is a good place for you, Taylor," she whispered.

He flinched, nearly hitting his head on the car door as he reeled away.

He could not see Eloise, but he heard her.

"Who is that?" he demanded.

Eloise turned off the car. The key pulled from the ignition and fell to the floor at his feet.

"A friend of Jasmine's," she answered.

Taylor lurched forward, scrambling for the keys. She forced her hand into his mouth, muffling the scream that came a moment later, and then pushed back. She slammed his head against the door until blood ran from the wound, matting his hair.

She held him there, one hand in his mouth and the other over his throat. All she had to do was push and wait. He kicked and wailed, the sound muffled and pathetic. His hands clutched at nothing; his feet stomped and flopped.

When he stopped, when he was dead, she stayed next to him in the car.

She stayed until it was almost dawn.

When she returned the next night, his car was gone. He was gone.

And she knew he would never return.

FAMILY MATTERS

Edgewood Cemetery was not far from the house on Berkley Street, but for some reason, Eloise couldn't go visit. She eventually decided it had to be the fence. It kept her out just as well as it had kept others in.

The fence around Edgewood Cemetery was made of wrought iron. So many old fences were designed that way, with intricate metalwork and spikes like little spears on top. Eloise sometimes wondered if they were made that way on purpose. Like battlements around a castle, had some living person realized that iron would keep the spirits at bay? Were cemeteries designed as prisons for the dead?

She had seen ghosts on the grounds over the years. Not many, rarely more than two or three at a time, but they were close, and they were unknown. That became something she could not ignore.

There were only so many people in Eloise's world. When the Andersons were gone, when the help all left the house and only the spirits remained, she could only do so much. Trying to have friends with Vivienne around had not been easy. She was as evil a thing as Eloise had seen.

But when Shane Ryan had gotten rid of Vivienne, it seemed like Eloise might have a chance to meet more people and make new friends. And she did, after a fashion. She met the Davis sisters. She met Frank and Tom. She even wandered the nearby neighborhoods as Nashua was swept up in the modern world and new cars and houses and people appeared.

But the cemetery had always remained out of bounds.

There was another reason the cemetery fascinated Eloise, of course. Her father was there. His ghost wandered the grounds of Edgewood from time to time, but she rarely saw him.

It was an autumn evening when Eloise found herself wandering near the cemetery again. The sun had just set, and the last light of day was barely more than a blue haze on the horizon.

The day was lost to a drizzle, and the living avoided it. Eloise enjoyed those days. The cold and wet meant nothing to her, but it gave her freedom. It made her feel like she was the only person in the whole world, and that she could go anywhere, even if only for a few moments.

"Are you Eloise?" a voice asked as she paced along the cemetery's iron fence, watching puddles grow as the misty rain filled them up.

The ghost was not much older than herself, Eloise thought, a fact that delighted her. Apart from Thaddeus, very few children were around, and even though she sometimes felt very old, she also felt the opposite just as often.

"I am. Who are you?" she asked.

The ghost stood on the opposite side of the fence in a pretty blue dress that was soaked down the front with something black. Her face was covered in blotches; angry, red spots that looked like a terrible rash, and her eyes were caked with yellow discharge. She had died of a sickness, though Eloise could only guess which one. She felt it might be rude to ask.

"My name is Adelaide," the ghost said.

Adelaide's dress and hair looked like they might have come from a time even before Eloise was born, but she had never seen the ghost. She must have been very good at hiding if she had kept out of sight for so long.

"I don't remember seeing you before," Eloise said.

The other girl shook her head.

"I don't enjoy coming out here very much. I like to be inside. There's a mausoleum just over there; do you see?"

She pointed to one of the bigger stone structures in the cemetery, and Eloise nodded. It had belonged to the Brewster family, and Eloise knew they were very rich, though she had never met any of them. She was certain the family had died out before her time.

"That's where I stay. I have more space than anyone here," Adelaide explained.

Eloise knew a brag when she heard it, but if the ghost did have a larger space than anyone else, maybe it was worth a boast.

"I am there," she replied, pointing to Shane Ryan's home.

"You live in the house?" Adelaide asked. "Not just on the grounds?"

"Yes. I only come out onto the grounds when I want to go for a walk."

"Is there someone alive there?" Adelaide asked.

"Oh, yes. Shane Ryan lives in the house."

"Has he ever seen you?" the other girl asked in a hushed tone as though they were now trading secrets.

"Shane Ryan sees me all the time. He's my friend, and we live together with the others."

"Oh," Adelaide replied. She did not seem enthused by the information, but Eloise did not see why. They had only just met, after all. They knew nothing about one another. Except…

"How did you know my name?" Eloise asked.

Adelaide smiled, and her teeth were caked with bits of whatever she had once vomited all over herself.

"Trevor told me. He talks about you sometimes," she explained.

Trevor was Eloise's father.

"You speak with my father?" she asked, somewhat confused by the news.

Eloise's father had once run a mill and had taken his work seriously. So much so, in fact, that his work life was much like his home life. He was in charge, and he was very strict. He made rules and schedules and expected them to be adhered to. He was not terrible, but he was not entirely warm, either. Eloise had learned much later that other fathers were more affectionate with their children.

"Oh yes, all the time. Sometimes he plays with me in the mausoleum and tells me stories about his life and the mill and you and your mother."

"Does he?" Eloise asked. It had been a very long time since she'd seen her mother. Sometimes it was hard to conjure an image of her. One day, memories of her would be gone entirely, Eloise thought, forgotten like so many other details from the past.

"We have so much fun together," Adelaide added.

Eloise did not want to acknowledge the twinge of jealousy she felt stirring inside, but it was difficult not to. She had experienced nothing like that with her father, even when he was alive. It was not comforting to know he was playing games with some stranger in his death.

"Is my father around?" Eloise asked, glancing out at the rest of the cemetery. She could see no other spirits.

"No, not right now," Adelaide answered without looking. "Do you know what he told me once?"

Eloise did not know, but she was beginning to not enjoy speaking with Adelaide. There was a smugness to her that Eloise found off-putting. She was not making a good first impression.

"He told me that he wished he had a daughter like me," the girl said. She grinned then and fell silent, staring at Eloise to gauge her reaction.

Eloise remained blank-faced. She blinked and regarded the other spirit flatly. She had been around long enough to know when someone was provoking her, but she did not understand why Adelaide would.

"Do you want to come play?" Adelaide asked after Eloise did not speak.

Eloise did not want to even speak to Adelaide anymore. She was becoming very objectionable. She wanted to see her father again, but getting into the cemetery was never a simple task without finding a creative way around the iron fence.

"There's no way in," Eloise pointed out.

"Don't be silly. Of course, there is. The side gate's been left open," Adelaide stated. "Come inside. Come see my home."

Eloise did as the other ghost asked and made her way around the edge of the fence until she found the small side gate. Eloise had never seen it left open, but it hung open now, the weeds around it trampled down.

She entered the grounds and walked back to Adelaide, who had not bothered coming to meet her. As soon as they were face to face, Adelaide turned her back and started walking.

"It's this way," she said, staying ahead of Eloise.

She led them past stones and monuments, and when Eloise caught up with her, she kept her eyes straight forward, not bothering to look at the other girl.

"How long have you been here?" Eloise asked, trying to remain civil.

"A very long time. My family is very old. We had deep roots in New England; did you know that? My father was a very rich man."

"I bet he was," Eloise said. She had no idea who Adelaide's father was, but a rich Brewster was not hard to imagine.

"Your father worked in a mill, didn't he?"

"He ran a mill," Eloise corrected.

"Of course. Did you ever go hungry?"

Adelaide did not turn her head when Eloise scoffed.

"I starved to death in a wall," she pointed out.

"Before that. Did you ever need to steal food? Did your father?"

"Of course not," she answered.

Adelaide grunted and stopped at the door of the large mausoleum she had claimed as her home. The doors were open and the stained-glass windows were broken, the shards all over the steps.

"What happened here?" Eloise asked.

"Some men broke in," Adelaide answered. "Look what they did."

Inside the mausoleum, the lid of a sarcophagus had been pushed to the floor, where it broke. Many things were broken, from the windows to the iron wall sconces.

Eloise drifted in and looked around the wide space. Vases for flowers were shattered, and a skeletal body lay disheveled and broken in the first ruined sarcophagus.

"They stole my mother's jewelry," Adelaide said. "Grave robbers. They stole everything. Except this."

Adelaide pointed to the door and a single gold necklace with a teardrop pendant that was stuck to the broken glass. In their haste, the robbers hadn't noticed it fall.

"Is that yours?" Eloise asked. Something about the necklace was out of the ordinary.

"Yes," the ghost replied. It was her haunted item, the thing that bound her to the cemetery. She had almost been stolen.

Eloise felt sympathy for the spirit now. She was certain it would have been a frightening prospect to have looters take you from your home.

"I'm sorry they did this," Eloise said.

"Who were they?" Adelaide demanded. She glared at Eloise, her expression grim.

"What do you mean?"

Adelaide's slap was so sudden that Eloise didn't see it coming. Her hand came out of nowhere and crossed Eloise's cheek. There was no pain, but it was a surprise.

"Who robbed my family?" Adelaide demanded, her voice bubbling with anger.

"Why would I know?" Eloise replied coldly.

"Why wouldn't you? These are your kind of people."

They stared at each other, and Eloise tried to fathom what the other ghost was suggesting.

"I'm not a thief," she said.

"But you know thieves. Low brow, low breeding, low class. Filth. Garbage. I mean, my word, just look at you. A filthy animal playing at being a girl."

"Me?" Eloise said, stunned. "You're no better."

The slap came from the other side this time. Eloise was more upset

58

that she hadn't seen it coming the second time than she was about it happening.

"Find my mother's jewelry or I will grind your father into dust, Eloise. I will make sure he stays down in the dark below this cemetery for eternity. Do you understand me?"

Adelaide was practically spitting, and Eloise felt her expression darkening. She felt like all the heat in the world was slipping away around her and the cold was freezing into a solid core within her chest.

"Where is my father?" she asked.

"Where I put him. Where he'll stay," Adelaide threatened.

She was the same as Vivienne, Eloise realized. This little girl was just like the girl in the pond. Just like Mr. Anderson, or some of the dark ones in the basement. She was made of hate and anger and thought she could bully others into doing whatever she wanted whenever she wanted.

Eloise wanted to tear the hair from the girl's head and strangle her with it, but she did not. She did not have to play the same game that Adelaide played. She knew better than that. There was no need to react harshly.

"Let my father go," Eloise said.

This time she caught the slap before it landed, catching the other ghost's wrist in the air. She gripped her arm.

Adelaide's expression twisted, and she grinned cruelly.

"Your father told me you are practically free and that you know this Shane person. Is he the thief?"

"He is not a thief," Eloise said.

"Prove it, or I'll have him buried in this cemetery alongside your father. If I were you, I'd move quickly."

Eloise felt her hands tense and tighten, realizing they had balled into fists. She forced them to relax, to unclench and loosen up as she backed away from the other ghost.

"I'm sorry you were robbed, Adelaide," she said. "But I don't know who did it. And I don't think I'll be looking for them."

A breeze kicked up in the cemetery, and leaves rushed into the open mausoleum.

"I hope you don't think I'm playing a game, little girl," Adelaide said coldly. "I am so much older than you. Don't try my patience."

"You invited me here to play though, didn't you?" Eloise asked. She took a step toward the door and found herself smiling. Her fingers extended, and the breeze grew stronger. That cold she felt building in her chest felt so much bigger, so much stronger now. She needed to maintain control.

"Do you want me to bury your friend Shane alive?"

"Do you want to visit the fence?" Eloise countered.

The question caught Adelaide off-guard. Eloise scooped up the golden teardrop pendant, smiled, and turned, letting loose a rush of freezing air as she ran from the mausoleum. Then, she flung the necklace toward the black-spiked fence that surrounded them.

The weight of the teardrop dragged the fine golden necklace until it snagged on the ironwork. Eloise ran back to the mausoleum and found the other ghost both upset and confused.

"What have you—" Adelaide began.

Her words were cut short by Eloise pushing her against the wall. The ghost fell back against one of the iron sconces and, in a blink, she was gone.

Eloise rushed outside then, toward the fence. The chain and pendant still hung on one of the iron spikes. Adelaide, thrust back to the pendant by the iron in the mausoleum, manifested in the gap between the iron bars of the fence and then vanished again, forced into the pendant once more.

The ghost appeared and vanished, appeared and vanished, over and over. The iron trapped her, preventing her from leaving the spot where her haunted item was now snagged.

She blinked in and out, sometimes long enough to make a faint noise or even lock eyes with Eloise. But only for a heartbeat. Only long enough for the iron to send her back again.

Eloise turned her back on the ghost.

"That seems cruel," a voice said. Eloise smiled as her father appeared.

"It does," she agreed.

It had been some time since she had seen her father. His face was not as she remembered it. Her memories were changing, she knew. Growing vague and unreliable.

"Are you well? I asked your friend Shane Ryan to say hello to you when last we spoke."

"I am. And he did."

Her father's face was broader than she remembered, like his nose. His jaw was too square, and his brown hair was cut short. Hadn't he been bald? Perhaps not.

"Was she keeping you trapped?" Eloise asked, indicating Adelaide.

Her father glanced at the ghost again, blipping in and out of existence on the fence. Around them, throughout the cemetery, other spirits began to rise.

"She was. Only recently. She was a Brewster, you see."

"I know," Eloise said. That was not a good explanation, she thought.

"They like things to go their way. Even now. Even here."

"Maybe this will change her mind," Eloise said.

Adelaide needed to learn manners. Eloise thought this was a good solution.

"Will you leave her this way? Forever?" Trevor asked.

"Someone will find the necklace soon enough. Someone who can move it."

There was no way for Eloise or the other spirits to move it now, of course. Not off the iron fence.

"I suppose you're right," her father agreed. He smiled then, and she remembered that. He had not smiled often, and so those memories were precious ones. "I'm glad you can stand up for yourself."

"Would you like to go for a walk?" she asked. It was still raining, and the gate was open. She was certain they would be able to go very far without seeing anyone.

"I would like that very much," he said.

She led them back to the gate that the thieves had left open, and out into the world beyond. The misty rain was silent, and the only sounds that followed them were the brief, staccato screams from Adelaide as she appeared and vanished over and over and over again.

THE STRANGER

The man in the parlor was going to die. Eloise could feel it in her bones. Not that she had bones anymore, but the expression was sound.

"Who is he?" Thaddeus asked.

He was Mr. Anderson's guest; that much was clear. He was seated in the parlor waiting to meet him and Mrs. Anderson, but there was something about him that Eloise found strange. The way he looked at the house, at the photos and the walls, was unusual. It seemed like he saw things other people didn't.

"Herr Hesselschwerdt," the butler said, entering the parlor with Mr. and Mrs. Anderson.

"Hair? His name is hair?" Thaddeus said.

Eloise shook her head.

"It's German. It just means 'mister'."

"Oh. What does Hesselschwerdt mean?"

"Names don't mean anything. What does Thaddeus mean?"

"My mother once told me it meant 'heart'," he answered.

"Shush. Come on."

New people did not often show up in the house. They hadn't for some time, anyway. Mr. Anderson's associates did sometimes, but the meetings were quick and clandestine, and Mr. Anderson made sure they left quickly.

Sometimes, Mrs. Anderson had people over for tea, but it had not happened nearly as often lately. Not since the dark ones in the root cellar had begun to creep about.

The ones in the cellar were not good. Eloise knew that, but she couldn't help feeling they hadn't always been bad. Or that they didn't mean to be that way. She knew they were hurting the servants. They had done terrible things. But they were just doing Vivienne's bidding. The girl in the pond. It was always her doing.

The strange man talked with the Andersons and left. He was set to return the next day, and Eloise wondered what sort of business he might be in. She did not like to spy on Mr. Anderson too closely. She didn't want him to catch her.

It was a strange feeling—fearing a living man—but she feared Mr. Anderson all the same. He could not hurt her, not anymore. But he could hurt others. He had hurt others. She knew some of his secrets.

The thing about secrets is that they were supposed to have two kinds of value. They were valuable kept or valuable told. Eloise had no one to tell Mr. Anderson's secrets to. And keeping them helped no one, so they had no value. They were just little horrors that she knew. Cruel things he had done. Terrible things.

Eloise kept them because she had no choice. She could not forget them. But one day, maybe, they would have value. If she found someone who could use them. Maybe the German was such a man. But maybe that was why she felt he would not live long. Maybe he would learn too many secrets. That was always a danger.

The servants murmured throughout the day about the stranger. They said he was a man who could talk to ghosts. Eloise found this very interesting, for most people did not like to talk to spirits. When she tried to talk to people, they were often very afraid, even when she was not trying to scare them.

They said the strange man was going to talk to the dark ones in the root cellar, and that was all Eloise needed to know. Her fears about the man's fate made sense. That was how he would die.

"Do you think he can talk to the dark ones?" Thaddeus asked. They were upstairs, between the walls, listening to the whispers of the house staff.

64

"No."

"But why would he say he could if it's not true?" the boy asked.

"Maybe it *is* true. But they won't talk to him."

Thaddeus never ventured below the house with her. He was afraid of the dark ones, even though Eloise was not. She kept her distance from them. She talked to them sometimes when they were willing, but she knew to avoid them when they were riled up like they were now. The stranger's arrival had gotten them very excited. Very angry. It was not a good time to be around them.

"What do you think they'll do?"

"Do you remember the gardener?" she asked in reply.

✳ ✳ ✳

Emily, one of the cooks, loved to make fun of Douglas the gardener. She was a foolish girl who was sharp-tongued and self-righteous. She mocked the others for their fear of the root cellar and its residents. And they heard her down there. They knew what she said, and they eventually punished her for it. She got off easily enough, only losing her eyesight. But Douglas wasn't so lucky.

Douglas went down to the cellar alone. Only Eloise and Thaddeus saw him go after Emily had left him. And only Eloise had followed.

"You should go back," she warned him as he crept down the ladder into the cold and dark, but he did not hear her.

Shadows raced around the man in the dark, and he froze in place. Eloise watched from the farthest corner, near the wall by the garden. She dared not intervene. It was not her place, and it would have changed nothing.

The dark ones scurried like rats sometimes; made themselves small. She wondered if that was on purpose. It confused the gardener and made him whip his head from side to side as sweat beaded his face despite the cold.

"Who's there?" he demanded.

"Who are you?" one of the dark ones replied in a deep, raspy voice.

"A fool," another answered for him.

"A dead man," said a third.

"Please," Douglas said.

One of the shadows slid up his spine. Eloise watched a dark, misty hand slip around the gardener's throat.

"Beg for your life," the shadowy spirit demanded.

"Beg!" echoed another.

"Beg for life."

Douglas gasped. He didn't get a word out. The pale flesh of his throat split and blood rushed out. Shadows ran through it, dashing back and forth. The blood splattered, and they laughed. They laughed as the life poured from him and his body slumped to the dirty floor.

None of them spoke as they dragged Douglas away. Inch by inch, his body was taken into the deepest darkness. Even Eloise could not see what they did there, but she heard the tearing and squelching. No one would find Douglas' body. No one would ever see him again.

* * *

Eloise followed the stranger around the house when he returned the following morning. Thaddeus came with her sometimes, and got bored and left at other times. She watched the man drink coffee and interview the staff and ask pointed questions in his amusing accent.

She watched him go from room to room, to see if anything was amiss. He was like a police officer, investigating the ghosts to learn of their crimes. But why had Mr. Anderson bothered to hire him in the first place?

The stranger eventually found his way to the butler's pantry with Mrs. Grady and Joan. Eloise knew what he planned to do. She watched him there, looking at that trapdoor with a silly expression like he was not walking into his death. She tapped on the wall to distract him.

"Hello?" the man said.

He turned to the two women with him and nodded. They left, closing the door behind him. Eloise watched him take a deep breath and search the room with his eyes.

"Hello?" he said again, this time more quietly. Eloise smiled. He was trying to be sly.

"Hello," she answered from the corner where she hid in the shadows.

She preferred the corners. It was always easy to slip up or down, left or right. She could be anywhere in an instant.

"Are you Eloise?" he asked.

She smiled at him.

"I am," she answered. "Why are you here?"

"To talk with you, and with Thaddeus," he answered. He had not tried to speak with either of them yet, of course. "And to speak with those in the root cellar."

Yes, that was the heart of it, Eloise thought. He was there to die. He could hear her; that part of his story was true. He could speak with the dead. But that was hardly going to help him in the root cellar. The dark ones didn't have much interest in talking, from what Eloise had seen. They wanted blood.

"Eloise?" the man said.

"Yes?"

"Who is in the root cellar?"

Your death, she thought. But instead, she gave him an honest answer.

"The dark ones," she whispered. She dared not risk letting Vivienne hear her. "Hers. You don't want to go in there. Stay up here and talk with me. Talk with Thaddeus. Talk with all of us."

She did not know this strange man and had no reason to care for him. But he seemed earnest. He was sincere in his desire to help. She had seen him with the servants. He'd listened to their stories about the house and their work. About the Andersons. He was not like the other people Mr. Anderson had brought to the house; the ones he called his business associates. This stranger was different.

"There are more of you?" the man asked.

"Of course," she said, laughing at the silly question. There were a lot of spirits in the house. "But don't go into the root cellar. They won't like you. She won't like it."

"Who is she?" he asked.

Eloise frowned. The last thing they needed to do was talk about Vivienne. Or mention her name.

"No," Eloise stated. "I don't want to talk about her. She doesn't like it."

If they started talking about her, she'd get angry. Everyone would suffer.

"Well, does she live in the house, too?" the man asked.

Eloise rolled her eyes in the darkness.

"No, but she decides what happens."

The man nodded and kept searching the room.

"Ah," he said. "But I do need to go down and talk to them."

"They may kill you," Eloise warned. She wasn't sure how else she could explain it. "They don't like people. They don't like anyone."

"Do you know who they are?" the man asked.

No one had ever cared to ask that. Eloise had, but they did not answer her. They were too angry. She wasn't even sure they knew who they were anymore.

"No," she said. "But I know when they came."

"When?" the man asked.

Eloise did not want to answer. She had been trying to distract him from them and from Vivienne. Keep him focused on talking to her and Thaddeus, not the dark ones.

"When did they come here, Eloise?"

"When the Andersons came," she whispered. They were Mr. Anderson's ghosts. She had seen the library. She had seen him creeping about and heard him talking. She didn't know all the details, but she knew that much. And maybe that would get this man killed if anyone found out what he knew.

"When the Andersons came, and Mr. Anderson put the books in the library. They came then, and they will not leave. The old man hates them. Thaddeus and I… we're afraid of them. And she… she loves them."

She let it all out in a rush. In for a penny, in for a pound was an expression she'd once heard. She didn't know why she told the strange man. Maybe to scare him off. Or maybe so that someone would know the secret, too. Know that the dark things in the cellar had come with Mr. Anderson. They were his dark secret. Maybe it was enough that the stranger would know before they killed him. She hoped he was smart enough to leave.

"Thank you, Eloise," the stranger said. He looked at the door in the floor and began to remove his cufflinks. Eloise sighed in the shadows. *What a foolish, foolish man*, she thought. She stayed still and silent as he opened the door and climbed down the ladder.

Eloise did not follow the man into the cellar. She had already seen them kill one person. She didn't need to see it again.

✳ ✳ ✳

"Mr. Hesselschwerdt," Thaddeus said. "He's still here."

Eloise looked at the boy, unsure of what he meant.

"His body?" she asked.

"Him," her friend replied. "The dark ones didn't kill him."

Eloise had not expected that. She was certain he would die. Maybe not totally certain, but he should have been maimed. Crippled or blinded or stricken with madness.

"Is he… well?"

"They didn't hurt him at all. I heard him in the parlor again with Mrs. Anderson."

They were between the walls where the sounds of the house were the quietest. Eloise had gone there to be alone because she'd felt sad for the stranger. Now, it seemed, those feelings were unnecessary.

But why had they let him go?

As if sensing her thoughts, something dark slipped through the cracks in the walls just behind Thaddeus. One of the dark ones was loose in the house, skulking about on the second floor. The farther the dark spirits went from the root cellar, the more Eloise worried. They only ventured so far when they had a purpose. Maybe letting the stranger go was part of some scheme.

She breezed past Thaddeus and followed the dark shape, traveling through walls and corners, trying to keep up with the flickering movements, but she lost it somewhere near the servant's quarters.

"Herr Hesselschwerdt," the butler yelled from below. "Upstairs!"

Eloise heard footsteps and a murmuring among the staff. She went through the passageways used by the servants and then out through a bedroom to a hallway, where she stopped in a corner as her eyes fell on the maid, splayed out on the floor as Mrs. Grady tried to revive her.

One of the dark ones slipped past her and Eloise followed suit.

"What did you do?" Eloise asked the spirit when she caught up with it in one of the upstairs rooms.

"What needs to be done, child. Stay away or suffer worse," it said in a voice like the creaking of a door hinge.

Someone rushed into the room—the stranger—and Eloise ducked below the bed, watching him as he confronted the dark one. He could see it, and speak with it, but he was not afraid. Eloise had not expected anyone to pursue the dark ones, especially not after meeting them. The stranger had many surprises, but he still played a risky game.

They parted ways, the dark one fleeing, and the stranger left alone. He returned to the hallway where Mrs. Grady was with the maid, alive though stricken by the spirit. In the blink of an eye, it had robbed her of her ability to bear children.

"Mrs. Grady, which room is the library?" the stranger demanded. Eloise shook her head. He did not want to go there. Mr. Anderson was there.

The servants tried to stall the stranger, and Eloise rushed past them, out of sight and desperate. She did not know what she could do, but she had to do something. Had to try something.

She entered the library, creeping in slowly from a corner and surveying the space. Mr. Anderson sat at a desk in near darkness, a single light shining on a display set before him. Jawbones were laid out on the desk, many of them, and he was using a cloth to polish their teeth while muttering quietly to himself.

Eloise wished she could kill him. It would be so much better if the world was free from such a man. But she was afraid of him.

The door opened, and the stranger barged in. Mr. Anderson looked up in surprise and Eloise shrank into the shadows. She was too late to save the stranger. Mr. Anderson would not like the man coming at him like this. Accusing him of things. Confronting him in his home. Why had he hired the stranger in the first place?

Mr. Anderson had a gun in his hands. Eloise had not seen him draw it. The stranger was calm, as though he'd had guns pointed at him before. He did not know what sort of man Mr. Anderson was.

I have to do something.

All she had to do was rush at him. Attack him. She could take away his gun. She could claw out his eyes. She could make him blind the way the dark ones did. She could save the stranger.

The men spoke, and for a time, Eloise thought it might be okay. Mr.

Anderson had not pulled the trigger. He might have only meant to scare the stranger.

Something in one of the bookcases clicked, and Mr. Anderson pulled it away from the wall. There was a door behind it. Eloise felt her stomach drop, even though she had no stomach left inside of her. She knew what was on the other side. She knew every inch of the house.

The man, the foolish stranger, did not fight. He did not run. Why wouldn't he fight?

Mr. Anderson came at him then and pushed him. The stranger stumbled through the door and fell into the hole. Eloise covered her mouth as she watched the man disappear into the hole and hit the bottom far below. She heard his bones break. She heard his scream.

Mr. Anderson continued to talk, to gloat about what he'd done, even as Eloise sank below the library, down into the stone. Down to the oubliette.

When Mr. Anderson had sealed the door and moved the bookcase, the stranger was alone. He was laughing now, for some reason. A sound that should have been so full of joy.

But all Eloise wanted to do was cry because she knew he would never leave that hole.

She wanted to cry, but she could not.

Check out these best-selling series from our talented authors:

GHOST STORIES

RON RIPLEY
BERKLEY STREET SERIES
MOVING IN SERIES
HAUNTED COLLECTION SERIES
DEATH HUNTER SERIES

IAN FORTEY
JIGSAW OF SOULS SERIES
CULT OF THE ENDLESS NIGHT SERIES

SUPERNATURAL SUSPENSE

A. I. NASSER
SLAUGHTER SERIES
SIN SERIES

DAVID LONGHORN
NIGHTMARE SERIES
ASYLUM SERIES

SARA CLANCY
THE BELL WITCH SERIES
BANSHEE SERIES

For a complete list of our new releases and best-selling horror books, visit ScareStreet.com or scan the QR code below!

Printed in Great Britain
by Amazon

57424473R00046